Expectations,
Great and Small

*Tales of encounters with life by characters
whose expectations are fulfilled or thwarted*

S.L.

Stanley Longman

EXPECTATIONS, GREAT AND SMALL

ISBN: 978-1-7364598-8-1

Printed in the United States of America

Published in the United States of America by Bilbo Books Publishing in Athens, Georgia.
www.BilboBooks.com
bilbobookspublishing@gmail.com
(706) 549-1597

COVER DESIGN BY GREGORY BOROKOWSKI
INTERIOR DESIGN BY TRACY COLEY

The stories in this collection display characters who experience life, bringing disappointment in some cases and fulfillment in others. We all live in a present time, cut off to a greater or lesser extent from the past, and uncertain about the future. There is no promise that what we expect is what will come to pass. There are occasions when one may feel without hope, only to find life suddenly and happily rewarding. Other times, the future brings a great disappointment.

There are ten stories here that may be divided into two categories. In one category, characters find their expectations thwarted. That happens to the couple whose marriage takes an unfortunate turn. One story has group of close friends celebrating the end of a pandemic that endured for so long, only to discover, quite suddenly, that it is not over. In another, an elderly woman lives a life that carries no cure for her loneliness. Still another portrays a man who chooses to dwell in his past, the present being so empty that he has no will to deal with it.

There are stories that that seem to promise new beginnings, as in the case of a little boy who tries to save the planet from the catastrophe predicted as the result of Global Warming. There is also a girl who gains satisfaction in saving a young boy.

A girl at a movie theater is sucked into a film to experience being saved by a matinee idol. On a still more positive note, a fat man, mocked in high school, finds a rewarding career. There is even a tale of an elderly couple with uncanny control over their lives. Finally, there is a boy who seems to meet Santa Claus.

Illustrations are by the author ("S.L.") and his talented granddaughter, Corah Longman ("C.L.").

Contents

At the Movies

A surreal experience

*E*very once in a while, the Pastime movie theater would schedule a whole Saturday afternoon of three full-length movies. They often had a common thread. They might all be western cowboy shows or military battle adventures or romances set on cruise ships. Lu Anne Newcomb liked going to these cinematic marathons, but she usually left soon after the third film was under way because, as she said, it's hard to sit for four hours or more. She would leave for home waving to her classmates still set to watch the third film.

One Saturday, however, she had reason to stay. The three films were to be all romances featuring that simply gorgeous young actor, Malcolm Rand. When she heard the news, she almost fainted. She could take four hours or more of Malcolm Rand. At lunch on Friday, she sat in the cafeteria with four other girls, all giggling in anticipation of the matinee the next day.

Ralph Tidrich overheard the girls chatter about Malcolm. He was a little older than Lu Anne but he "sort of" liked her. He stopped her in the hallway when classes changed and he asked her if he could have a date with her at the Pastime for the matinee on Saturday. She said "Sure!" He promised to meet her at her house, only a few blocks from the movie house, and they could walk there together.

All went according to plan. Ralph bought two tickets at the box office. They entered the house and found two seats together. Ralph went back to the refreshment counter and bought a tub of popcorn. He passed it to Lu Anne and took his seat next to her just as the lights were going down. When the MGM Lion roared at them from the screen, he reached down to hold

C.L.

S.L.

her hand. She passed him the popcorn tub, causing him to release her hand to get hold of the tub. Later, when he attempted to put his arm around her shoulder, she leaned forward suddenly and his arm dropped down. Meanwhile the tub kept being passed back and forth. Finally, Ralph gave up, slouched down and watched the sweet movie in boredom.

Some time into the second film, Ralph looked over at Lu Anne and saw her on the edge of her seat, her attention riveted on the images of Malcolm Rand on the screen. "Excuse me," he said, trying to pass in front of her and into the aisle. She barely moved, but he made his way in front of her into the aisle and out of the theater. The tub of popcorn stayed with her.

The third film came on the screen and she noticed that Ralph had not come back. She shrugged and leaned forward anticipating the moment Malcolm Rand would appear. The opening scenes were long shots of a crowded battlefield with horses galloping, canons booming, guns popping, and banners waving. Despite the noise, Lu Anne found it a little tiresome. She wanted Malcolm to appear. She slouched and finished the popcorn. She began to nod off. A horse and rider ran directly at her, and then veered off to the left. That woke her up. She noticed a house on fire in the distance, but still, no Malcolm Rand while more horses ran by. She fell asleep.

Suddenly, she thought she heard her name. Malcolm was looking directly at her, his face occupying the entire screen. She jolted awake and saw Malcolm disappear below the screen and re-appear in the aisle below. He ran to her, pulled her from her seat, took her in his arms and ran back down the aisle. The two showed up immediately on the screen.

He was carrying her out of the flames of the burning house. She clasped her arms around his neck as he ran away from the house toward his horse. He gently lifted her onto the saddle. Before he could swing himself up on the horse's back, he saw an enemy soldier running at him, his saber drawn. Lu Anne watched as the two engaged in a wild sword fight. For a while, Malcolm seemed to have been beaten back into some bushes. But then, with a sudden burst of energy, he rushed toward his adversary and thrust his sword into his belly. The man gasped and fell to the ground. Malcolm watched him squirm in agony and he prepared to deliver a death thrust. Before he could do so, the man made one last jerk and lay still.

Malcolm said to Lu Anne, "We have to get you away from here. This battle is still in full vigor." With that, he swung himself onto the horse's back. Lu Anne held tightly to his waist and he rode off taking her over the crest of a nearby hill. There, he helped her down off the horse. The noise of the battle cannons and guns was muted in that place. "You'll be safe here. I'll be back." With that, he was gone.

Lu Anne stood there watching him ride back into battle. She swooned and fell to the ground. When she came to, she heard an explosion from the field followed by a gradual brightening of the sky.

She awoke. She saw the words "THE END" projected on the screen. The house lights were coming on. People were walking up the aisle. With the words, "Excuse us," couples in her row were asking to slip by her. After a moment she recognized what they asked and shifted position to let them by. Slowly, she managed to shake off the battlefield and the face of Malcolm Rand. She was the last to leave the movie theater. She was startled to go out into the late afternoon sun.

C.L.

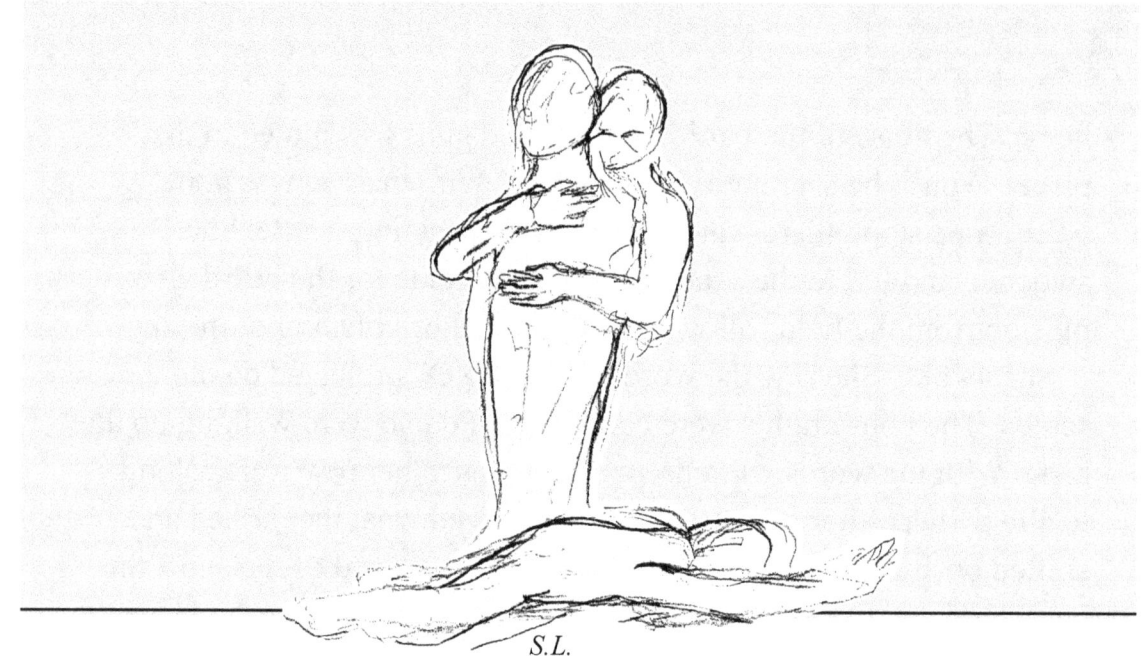

S.L.

Married Life

In two installments

C.L.

𝒴ears ago, in 1961, Sam and Melanie Pritchett passed through their days of courtship with a kind of startled wonder. Two years later, that wonder translated into a wedding, followed by a honeymoon during which they celebrated each other in every way imaginable. After another two years, a baby boy came into their life. They named him Gregory. Growing up, he proved to be a talented musician, capable of playing several different instruments. He went on to graduate from college with a degree in music. He soon was attracting notice as a composer. Gregory Pritchett was becoming a name to be reckoned with.

As time passed, he gave his parents more and more cause to take pride in their son. Then, quite suddenly, a dark cloud covered the sunshine of their life. They were summoned to confirm the identity of a body believed to be that of Gregory Pritchett. They went at once and, to their horror, discovered that the body was indeed Gregory's. He had died of an overdose of opioids. They knew he had experimented with drugs, but they never expected this devastating news. The shock plunged them into deep grief. They threw themselves into each other's arms, each sensing the suffering of the other. Their shared compassion helped them as they went into intense mourning.

Friends and relatives came to offer condolences. As those condolences gradually subsided, a strange twist grew in their grief, causing them to shift their attention from Gregory to one another. This did not have to happen. Someone should have stepped in and stopped it. That someone should have been the other. "Why didn't you do something? You knew he was into drugs." "How was I to know it was this serious?" "You knew he was experimenting. That should have alerted you," and "You knew as much as I did, but you let it go." These, and many more recriminations, piled up until the marriage itself was collapsing.

Before it could collapse, however, a new wrinkle developed. They were in their eighties. Melanie began to notice that Sam was saying and doing peculiar things. He repeated statements two or three times in a row. He wandered this way and that. Melanie found his behavior irritating and she told him so. Her reproof did not faze him. He declared he needed a certain item and started to look for it, only to forget what he was looking for. One time, he opened a closet door, walked in, stayed there a while and then finally came back out. Worse and more alarming was when he went out and was found wandering two blocks away.

He was diagnosed with Alzheimer's. Melanie felt obligated to see him through, but it only got worse. Eventually, she had to give up and placed him in a nursing home. She would visit him there from time to

S.L.

time. Eventually, she gave up. He no longer recognized her. There was no point in trying to think of their having any relationship.

He was gone without going anywhere.

The afternoon of her last visit, she came home to an empty house. Of course, it was not really empty - there were any number of items (photos, glasses, books, clothing) to remind her of him. She felt a rush of different emotions. She sensed a great relief. A heavy burden had been lifted. She had felt lonely, but now, this was absolute loneliness. She threw herself onto the couch and sighed deeply. Then, she noticed on the side table a framed photo from their wedding. She picked it up and studied it. Tears welled up in her eyes. She turned the photo face down and she wept.

C.L.

A day in the life of
Millicent Devries

*M*illicent DeVries was on the verge of becoming a woman. At school, most girls were ahead of her. It bothered her, but at the same time, she did not like the changes she had begun to sense with her body. Her mother had tried to reassure her, but she remained uncomfortable. To make matters worse, she knew she had been tagged a "Plain Jane" at school. The one thing she liked was taking long walks away from anyone else. One time out on a long walk, she passed some of her giggling classmates and heard one of them call out to her, "Hey, you! Yeah, you! I betcha you're always pretty cold with a name like Milly Deepfreeze" and the gaggle of girls shrieked with laughter. She held her head up high and walked on. She really did not like any of her classmates, and she also began to feel that she did not even like herself.

She was in that frame of mind one afternoon when she walked into the upper level of the city park. There was a retaining wall that divided the park into upper and lower levels. She noticed a boy seated on the edge of the wall, looking out over the lower park. He had his back to her so she could easily slip by him without his noticing. She didn't much like boys any more than giggling girls. Boys often behaved like bullies.

Once she got past him, she stopped and looked back. He seemed to be sobbing. She listened closely and saw that his entire body was shaking. She watched him for a while. Then she approached him slowly. Indeed, his sobs were racking his whole body. He did not notice her and she hesitated. She thought maybe it would be better to leave him alone. She started to turn away, but something caused her to stop. She approached him, held out her hand and touched his shoulder. He jumped and started to fall forward. She grabbed him around his waist and they both fell backward. They lay there for a while, trying to catch their breaths. Then they turned toward each other. She saw the tear-stained face of a boy a few years younger than she. Suddenly, she burst into laughter causing him to say, simply, "What?"

"Don't you see? You aren't weeping anymore. This scare made you stop."

They thought about that as they lay on their backs at the top of the wall. Finally, she broke the silence by asking, "Why were you crying anyway?"

"'Cause I'm no good."

"What makes you say that?"

"My Daddy told me so."

"Why do you think he said that?"

"Because I sassed my Mom."

"What did you say to her?"

There was a long silence while the boy started tearing up. Finally, he explained between gasps, "I told her that I thought the stuff I was supposed to eat was awful. Then I slammed my fork down on the table. That's when Daddy stood up and pulled me out of my chair and put me in the corner of the living room." The boy stopped for a moment, then continued, "He said I was no good and didn't deserve to be in the family, ever!"

Millicent said, "I'm sure he didn't mean it."

"He meant it all right. I snuck out of the house, jumped on my bike and pedaled away as fast as I could." Again he gasped. "I was going so fast coming into the park that I fell and the bike went over the wall. It's down there somewhere. I'm no good."

Millicent stood up and looked down on the boy. "What's your name?"

"Nathanial Potts. And I hate it."

"I'm Millicent DeVries. And I hate it."

That caused the boy to give a short laugh. "I sometimes call myself Nate. It's a little better."

"I sometimes call myself Milly. It's a little better. Look, Nate, you stay here and I'll go get your bike." Nate stood up and watched her go to the far end of the wall and turn into the lower park. He went to the edge of the wall and saw her pick up the bicycle and wheel it back to the boy.

Once there, Milly said, "Now, Nate, let's go home."

"They don't want me there."

"Do you know what an apology is, Nate?'

"It's sort of 'I'm sorry,' isn't it?"

"That's what you are, right?"

Nate nodded. The two of them started walking with the bicycle, as Nate gave directions to his house. Once there, Milly rang the doorbell and stood back. She watched a woman come out the door and take Nate up in her arms, holding him tightly. A man joined them. Nate pulled away enough to point at Milly, saying,

C.L.

"That's Milly. She's my friend." All three looked at Milly. The man smiled and walked over to her. With a tear in his eye, he thanked her for bringing Nathanial home. Then he asked her name. "I'm Millicent DeVries." Nate said loudly, "She wants to be called Milly!" The father asked where she lived, thanked her again so very much for bringing Nate home. He wheeled the bike into the garage. Nate waved to Milly and the family went inside.

Millicent turned and started toward home. She thought to herself how good the family must feel to have everyone together again. As she walked along, it occurred to her that she rather liked herself. Perhaps the name Millicent DeVries wasn't so bad after all.

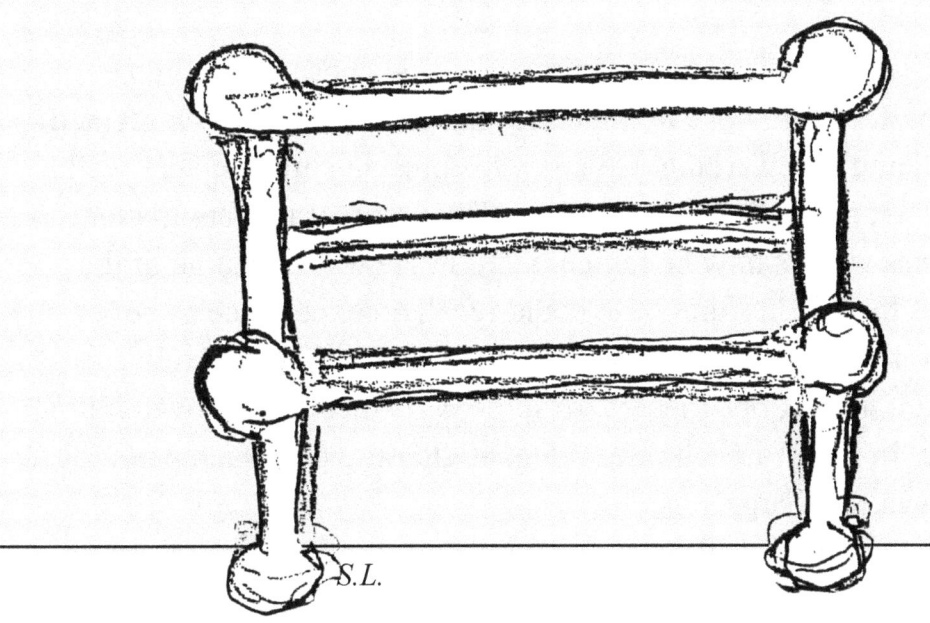

S.L.

No life
left to live

*B*ruce Cahill lived several years ago. He chose to live in the past. He did not care much for his present life, which seemed to him dull and unrewarding. He knew his present situation very well and it was not promising for the future. The past was another matter. The past was always how he remembered it. He was in charge of the past. It was his and his alone. He could recall an experience as he pleased. If it happened to be a pleasant experience, he could relive that pleasure. Inevitably, there were some parts that had annoyed him at the time. In such cases, he was adept at glossing over such parts. Again, he was in charge.

Some memories played out in his mind very briefly, others were terribly complex. Late one afternoon, for example, he sat in his favorite easy chair viewing the shadows created by the setting sun. It reminded him very briefly of a moment when his granddaughter played among those shadows, jumping from one to another. It made him smile.

On one occasion, he was walking in the city park when he came upon a park bench. It brought back to mind a whole series of events, leading up to a mutual declaration of love on a park bench. He sighed. A memory may inspire joy and yet carry a sadness born of its being lost in time. It cannot be relived. He had a good marriage, but there always remain some regrets. Regrets can still float in the mind but one cannot go back and resolve them. Some few years ago, his dear wife died.

That led to the one memory he really could not control. It was the grief that lodged itself in his mind. He relived those moments watching her die over and ever. He recalled awakening to see her sitting on the edge of the bed. He heard her say, "It hurts." He went to her and held her. Then she was gone.

After that, those regrets can never be resolved. Even though years have passed, he continued to call up the joys and sorrows they shared.

The more he indulged in his past, the more he became stymied in the present.

A voice in his head told him that all he had was the reality of the present moment. He knew that. Yet, he could never quite shake off the paralysis induced by his constantly returning to his past life, as if there were no life left to live.

C.L.

Bernie
saves the planet

*B*ernie Whitaker was a committed and compassionate fellow. Whenever he would find a situation harmful to somebody, he would look for ways to intervene. He didn't often find a way. After all, he was only six. One development was so dire that he resolved to throw all his energy to counteract its effects. Indeed, it could spell disaster for the entire planet. Even his Mom and Dad might perish.

It came to his attention one afternoon when he spread himself out on the living room floor playing with his toy cars. His parents and a guest were in a discussion sounding very serious, so much so that Bernie started listening. At first he heard snippets of the conversation: "The earth is warming at an alarming rate," "They say we have little or no time to stop a catastrophe," "We're already seeing huge storms develop and they are more frequent and more destructive than ever before." Bernie quit playing with his toys and just listened. Then someone said, "This could very well destroy life on the entire planet." Another said, "It may already be too late to save the planet." The conversation carried on and no one noticed how intently Bernie was listening. He left the room unobserved.

He went to his room. There, he started laying plans. Something had to be done. Those old people won't be around when the time comes and the earth suffers its horrible end. He'll have to deal with this coming disaster and hope his example will inspire other young ones. He did not use those terms exactly, but he did understand that gasses were getting trapped above us. That meant that heat cannot escape and that's causing something called "Global Warming." He did not know just why that meant disaster for the planet. He did know that something had to be done to stop it from happening. And it had to be done right now.

Bernie went to work on the problem. He reasoned that what had to happen would be to make an opening up there in the sky to let the gasses out. The problem was, he thought, "How do I get up there to make that hole in the sky?" That's not all. Once there, he'd need some tool to make the hole. This, he said to himself, is not going to be easy, but it is urgent.

Bernie took up pencil and paper. He would make a plan. He knew he needed a plan. He also knew he needed to find materials. In fact, he knew he couldn't make a plan without knowing what materials he had. He went straightway to the garage where he found a fine piece of plywood about three feet square. Looking around, he spied an old child's rocking chair he once used. He tried it on. He could still sit in it. He thought and thought: what if he attached the chair to the plywood? Then he could ride the chair up into space. He looked all over the garage. At last he spied a long rope. That's it! He would use the rope to tie the chair to the plywood. He drew a picture of the chair on its plywood platform,

Bernie felt like he was making real progress. The next thing, he thought, was some sort of machine that could blow a hole in the sky. He could not find anything in the garage. How about in the basement? He ran into the house and down into the basement. There, in the far corner, was an electric fan. That might blow a hole in the sky, especially if it were set on high speed. He had better test it, he told himself. He plugged it in and punched the lever to high speed. It worked perfectly! Very pleased, he took it out to his "space chair." He had just enough rope left to tie the fan down by its neck.

At that point, Tom Carson stopped to watch him at work. Tom, who lived two doors down from Bernie's house, was twelve years old, just twice Bernie's age. After watching a while, he asked, "Hey, kid, what is that thing?"

"It's what I am going to use to save the planet."

"That will save the planet?"

"Yeah. See, the problem is that gasses are blocking air and everything is getting warmer."

"Why's that bad?"

"It makes big storms."

Tom smirked, "Oh? So, how's this thing supposed to stop that from happening?"

Bernie tried to be patient. "Look. I am going up in the sky and blow a hole that will let those gasses get out. I got it all worked out, see?"

"You going to use that fan to blow the hole?"

"Yep."

"How you gonna plug it in, up there in space? You got a socket in the sky?"

Bernie was crestfallen. He didn't know what to say.

"Tell you what, kid. I'm gonna help you, seeing as how you're saving the earth. I got a fan works on a battery. You don't hafta plug it in. I'll let you use that. But hey, you got another thing to think about. I'll tell you what it is. It's propulsion."

"What's poaposhun?"

"It's what pushes you forward, up into the sky. You gotta have that. I got something. Wait here, kid. I'll go get that thing and I'll get the battery fan, too." Saying that, he ran off,

Left behind, Bernie began to feel dubious. Maybe this is not a good plan, he thought to himself. He hadn't thought of "poaposhun." He really did not know how he would get the thing on its way to the sky. He went on muttering to himself about this oversight.

Tom Carson came back. He handed a hand-held, battery-operated fan to Bernie. Then he produced what looked like a long stick, saying, "This is for your propulsion. Look. I'll tape it on the back of your chair and then I'll light it, and then, BOOM, off you go."

Bernie smiled broadly. "What is that thing, anyway?"

"Oh, it's just something I picked up last July fourth. You know, a kind of fireworks."

"How you going to light it?"

"I got a match. You ready to fly?"

Bernie settled into his rocking chair, grabbed the fan with one hand and the arm of his chair with the other. "Shoot!" he exclaimed.

Tom started to do the count down, starting with ten. When he got to zero, he struck the match and lit the stick and ran away some distance. He turned back to watch the sparklers spray over Bernie's head. He laughed loudly and ran home.

Of course, Bernie just sat there. The sparkler came to a stop. He could hear Tom's laughter fade away. Then a tear filled his eye. And a tear filled the other eye. He began to sob. He threw the fan to the ground and wept.

Mrs. Whitaker looked out the kitchen window and saw her son Bernie sitting in the little rocking chair on top of that piece of plywood. When she went out to ask him what he was doing, she noticed at once that he was weeping bitter tears.

She knelt beside him. "What is wrong? Why are you crying?"

Between sobs, Bernie said, "I couldn't do it. I tried, but I couldn't do it."

"What did you try to do, dear Bernie? Tell me."

"I tried…I wanted to save the planet. I needed to do that for you and for Dad."

"What do you mean, save the planet?"

Bernie explained to his mother that something had to be done and it had to be done right away, otherwise life will stop. He added, "You and Dad will go first because you're older."

She helped him out of his little rocking chair and clasped him closely. She realized what it was that Bernie was talking about. She assured him that there were people seriously at work on saving the planet. He did not have to do it all by himself. Then she looked down on the plywood and the little rocking chair and asked, "What have you put together here?"

"That's what I'll use to go up and blow a hole in the sky."

"And what's this stick?"

"That? Tom gave me that. He said it would give me poaposhun. But it didn't work. It just set off a bunch of sparks. It was no good."

Mrs. Whitaker thought she might have to have a few words with Mrs. Carson. Then she took little Bernie inside and washed his tear-stained face. She told him she was proud of him. He tried to do something really important.

Hearing that, Bernie smiled.

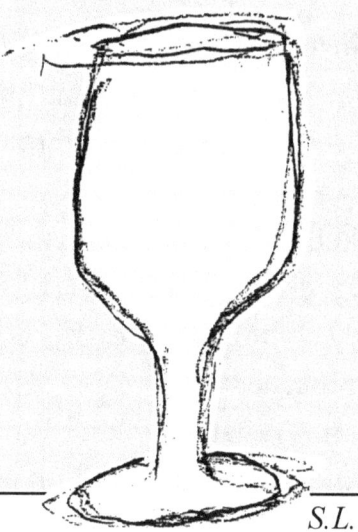

S.L.

A Post-Pandemic

Dinner Party

George and Marjorie Du Pré

The Invitation

After months of "self-isolating," "sheltering in place," "social distancing," wearing masks and washing hands, a group of old friends received an invitation to share a festive dinner, hosted by George and Marjorie Du Pré. Marjorie, a genteel Southern lady, had formed this circle of friends, and she sent the invitations, as she had done many times before. Her invitation instructed everyone that they would be participating in a ritual to celebrate victory over the virus. Accordingly, the guests were to bring all their leftover masks. They would be used in a ritual designed to symbolize the defeat of COVID-19. Actually, there had not been a full eradication of the virus, but people were so weary of enduring lonely, unvaried days, they declared the pandemic had run its course. They sent their RSVPs, anticipating a jolly evening as life was returning to normal.

The Friends

George and Marjorie's marriage had been arranged. Marjorie Du Pré started life as Marjorie Sutton Elsberg Harrington. The Harringtons and the Du Prés were prominent in the community, and this marriage could pool their prestige and financial prowess. To speed things along, George, who was a realtor, happened to represent another prominent family that had fallen on hard times and needed to sell their antebellum mansion on Lake Street quickly.

Tabitha Garner

George worked out the deal, bought the house and presented it to Marjorie as a wedding present. Two months later, she settled in as the lady of the house. She did all the things a genteel lady of means would do: she sponsored charity balls, organized tea clubs, and supported the local Museum of Fine Art. What's more, she also arranged festive musical and dramatic entertainments. Her dinner parties became a source of pride for her, and a source of envy for those not invited. At the time of the post-pandemic dinner party, she and George had been married for thirty-seven years, and George had learned to stay out of the way.

George Evan Du Pré was a realtor. He was always quiet and reticent, almost unobtrusive in social situations. There was something solid and dependable about him. It was this quality that sustained his marriage with Marjorie. He happened to be quite successful in the real estate business. He easily gained the trust of his clients and indeed he served them well. Quiet as he was, he harbored a deep current of humor. In fact, he rather relished Jeannie Grayson's giggling amusement about everything. Of course, he did not giggle, but he often chuckled inwardly. He brought Floyd Henry Robertson into the circle of friends after arranging a land purchase on which Floyd Henry built a new supermarket.

At the time of the dinner party, Tabitha Garner had been a widow for nearly twenty years. She was just eighteen years old when she married Leo Garner, twelve years her senior. Their relationship was always part husband-wife and part father-daughter. It was not an unhappy marriage. Still, she felt a certain sense of liberation after his death. With a very nice inheritance, she created a business of her own: a fashionable ladies' dress shop. Within a few short years, the shop became a highly profitable enterprise. She made periodic trips to New York, Paris or Milan for the fashion shows. She herself dressed elegantly. This combination of success and elegance attracted a number of suitors. She played with them as a cat plays with a mouse. This way, she maintained her independence. Marjorie Du Pré was one of her regular customers. Eventually, she made Tabitha one of her particular friends, regularly invited to join the other friends to the grand dinner parties at the Du Pré mansion on Lake Street.

For many years, Harold Grayson assisted Marjorie with her investments. He was not only a banker, but also a financial advisor. He managed her money well and she had an excellent portfolio. It is also true that the small percentage he skimmed off each new investment served him very well. While he was essentially humorless, he valued his friends and cared about their wellbeing. This may explain his forbearance with his wife's giggling.

When Jeannie married Harold, people thought it the most improbable bond, one finding amusement in everything and the other, in nothing. Perhaps that was the key, each needing a little of what the other had. At any rate, Jeannie came to Harold's attention on a particular day that neither of them will ever forget. It was raining and both were rushing toward each other, their umbrellas obscuring their view ahead. They collided. Jeannie plopped down in a puddle. Harold rushed to her aid but stopped short on hearing her laughing uncontrollably. Then he helped her to her feet, she still laughing, and he feeling concern. That combination has seen them through their marriage. At that time, Jeannie was working as a receptionist in a doctor's office. The doctor

Harold & Jeannie Grayson

felt that her humor was actually helping his patients and was disappointed when her wedding to Mr. Grayson caused her to resign.

One afternoon, George drove Marjorie to the General Hospital. She walked to the Technology and Radiology Division and it was there that she met Frank Shine. Her doctor had ordered some tests, one of which was a full body scan. Frank was the technician who helped her through the process, and he sensed her anxiety. The very idea of being sent into that dark narrow tunnel caused her to imagine the horror of being crushed or simply getting stuck in there. Frank sat with her for a long while to reassure her that it would be perfectly safe. It all went well, and she emerged much relieved. George was to meet her at the hospital's South Portal when she summoned him on her cell phone. Frank had her settle into a wheelchair and wheeled her to the portal. While they waited, she became curious and asked, in all innocence, "Now, what is it like to be a Negro?" A little startled, Frank began to talk. He

Frank Shine

told her how writers and poets reflected on their lives during the Harlem Renaissance, the Civil Rights Movement and the present day. In the midst of that, George called on the cell phone that he was waiting to have the car jump-started. By the time George finally drove up, she had heard about authors such as Langston Hughes, James Baldwin, Douglas Turner Ward, Toni Morrison and August Wilson. Marjorie was impressed and asked George to get Frank's phone number so she could invite him to one of her dinner parties.

Floyd Henry Robertson

Floyd Henry Robertson was always pleased to present himself using his triple-barrel name. He considered it his due, having come up from stock-boy at a local grocery to the owner of a chain of supermarkets that he called "Floyd's Bounty." He was proud, but at the same time he retained that stock-boy awkwardness. So it came as a surprise to be included in one of the Du Prés' dinner parties. George had found in him a kindred spirit, both feeling some of the same unworthiness. They also tended to enjoy the same jokes and stories. Indeed, it was only in the company of Floyd Henry that George laughed out loud. On the other hand, Floyd Henry tended to be a little too jovial. George persuaded

Helen Griswold

Marjorie to invite him to one of their dinner parties, pointing to the man's success with his many "Floyd's Bounty Supermarkets."

The guests at the dinner parties enjoyed the many contributions Helen Griswold made for their entertainment. She was a true dilettante, dabbling in many art forms. She picked up a variety of musical instruments, took to writing poetry, sketched many nature scenes, and was always at work on her novel. One day, Tabitha saw her seated on a fold-up canvas chair, intently drawing in her sketchbook. She struck up a conversation about her many artistic endeavors. Helen mentioned that she had taken up the fipple flute and had come to the point of playing it rather well. That led Tabitha to urge her to come and play at one of the dinner parties. Marjorie was delighted with the idea and sent her an invitation. People were intrigued by the prospect of hearing a fipple flute. They remained curious, even after Tabitha said it was also called a recorder.

Cocktails Before Dinner

The evening was to begin in the great drawing room for pre-dinner drinks. Everyone knew this. After all, that was protocol from the days before the plague and it needed to be re-established.

The guests were to arrive at 5:30. Unlike their dinner parties from before the pandemic, when they sauntered in over a half hour, this time, they arrived almost in unison, right at the appointed time. They were almost giddy with delight at seeing one another. George Evan Du Pré greeted them and methodically moved among them getting their drink orders. The task was not easy because they were all chattering loudly, one conversation piling over another with sudden bursts of laughter. George could scarcely get anyone's attention to take drink orders. People started making their own drinks, so he gave up and settled into his favorite chair. From there, he heard one snippet of conversation in one part of the room followed by a snatch of a sentence from another, a chortle in the far corner, and a guffaw from the drink table. This is some of what he heard: "You remember Patrick, the fellow who…" "Now let me tell you what I heard…" "It was so funny, I just had to laugh…" (followed by a hearty laugh)…"Tell me, who would have predicted 2020 would be…?" And so on.

Suddenly, Marjorie Du Pré clapped her hands. The chatter stopped and the room fell silent. Everyone turned toward Marjorie standing in front of the fireplace. Once she had their undivided attention, she spoke: "Ladies and gentlemen, the time has come. George and I extend a warm welcome to you all…" Hearing these words, George leapt to his feet and joined her. She waited a moment and then continued. "George and I have prepared a special delight for you, our long-time friends, haven't we, George?" George nodded. She continued, "Now, we want you all to form a big circle here in front of the fireplace. I hope you remembered to bring your used masks. Have them at the ready." Everyone obligingly formed a circle. Jeannie Grayson skipped to her place in the circle, giggling and saying, "Oh, what fun! I mean, really!" And Floyd Henry Robertson smiled and replied, "Oh, Marjorie always has something up her sleeve." Tabitha Garner simply smiled in her good-natured way and took her place in the circle.

"Now," Marjorie continued. "George is going to light the gas logs in the fireplace while you all begin rotating clockwise in front of the fire, stopping just to throw your face masks into the fire and then moving on." Everyone followed those directions. Once George lit the fire, the circle rotated and people began making witty remarks. Frank Shine chanted, "Eenie, meenie, minie mo, catch a BIGGER by the toe. If he hollers, let him go!" That caused uproarious laughter. The circle rotated two more times as they watched their masks go up in flames. At the end, they scattered, still laughing — everyone but Harold Grayson, who muttered, "Stuff and nonsense!"

George then turned off the gas logs. Marjorie announced dinner was about to be served and asked the group to move to the dining room. She informed them that they should look for their nametags placed at the table. She turned to George and asked him to alert the kitchen staff that it was time to start serving. The guests left their glasses on the drink table and moved into the dining room, as instructed.

At Table

Marjorie had made sure that everything was done properly and elegantly. It was to be a three-course dinner. She hired an Italian chef and two servers. Those two had earlier used a measuring stick to lay out the table with exactitude. One server took care of the water and wine glasses, and joined the other serving dishes for each course. Marjorie had a button at her foot to buzz the kitchen and summon the servers when needed.

Everyone took his or her place at the table according to this assignment: At the foot of the table sat Marjorie and to her right along one side sat Harold Grayson, Frank Shine, and Tabitha Garner while George sat at the head of the table and to his right sat Jeannie Grayson, Floyd Henry Robertson and Helen Griswold.

Once they were all settled, Helen Griswold stood up to make an announcement. "During this pandemic, I have taken up painting in watercolors. Before we break this evening, I want to take a few group shots of our wonderful set of friends. I will take those shots home and use them to do a painting in watercolors, I hope it will in a way memorialize our warm and enduring fellowship." The others clapped with approval.

Floyd Henry Robertson jumped to his feet saying, "I propose a toast to our wonderful hosts, Marjorie and George!" With that he held up his empty glass. Marjorie pointed out that the wine had not yet been served. "Before anything else, we must have the blessing." With that, she turned to George.

George picked up the cue. While the guests bowed their heads, he spoke these words: "Dear Lord, our God and Father, we humbly thank you for seeing us through this time of great fear and worry. It is through your love and abundant care that we now relish a new life with a new freedom and new choices. In Jesus Christ's name we pray. Amen." Marjorie beamed her approval and pushed the button to alert the kitchen staff.

The servers entered. This meal was a culinary delight based on the best Italian cuisine. The appetizer consisted of prosciutto and cantaloupe, then came a pasta dish, farfalle alla bolognese, and the main course, veal wrapped in bacon (saltimbocca alla romana) with a vegetable. This was topped off with coffee and a delicious tiramisu for dessert. With each new dish, Jeannie Grayson giggled with wonder and Tabitha gasped with delight. Even Harold Grayson was seen smiling. Floyd Henry Robertson saw his glass was full and again offered a toast to the hosts. Marjorie and George acknowledged the toast graciously.

At the end of the meal, Helen Griswold took her camera and went to one end of the table. "Now," she said. "I'll take few shots of you happy people and use them when I paint my memorial watercolor." The guests arranged themselves and put on happy faces. She took several shots, then looked at the camera window. There she saw something that startled her. She looked up at the people and back at the camera and again at the people. She stared at Frank Shine. "Frank! Are you all right?"

Frank coughed. He replied, "Well. I'm not sure. Let me ask a question. I have been wondering as I ate why those wonderful dishes did not taste as good as they looked. Then came the dessert. Did anyone notice that it had no flavor — no flavor at all?"

"It was delicious!" retorted Floyd Henry Robertson.

"Oh my, yes!" said Jeannie Grayson, giggling.

Frank covered his mouth and coughed again.

There was a long silence. Then Harold Grayson took his wife's arm, saying, "Jeannie and I really have to go. Thank you for the wonderful dinner. Come, Jeannie." They left.

Suddenly, goodbyes were uttered all around and the other guests left. Frank was the last to go. On his way out, he turned to George and said, "Guess I'm the Bigger and they caught my toe." And he was gone.

Marjorie opened the door to the kitchen and told the chef and the servers they were free to go. They were puzzled and asked why. Marjorie replied, "It's for the best. Don't worry. I'll clean up."

Marjorie and George worked together clearing the table and washing the dishes. All the while, they each had a worry they left unsaid.

Epilogue

In the following weeks, Frank got very sick. He was taken to the hospital and put on a ventilator. Helen finished her watercolor painting of the group, a painting she intended as a way to memorialize that dinner party. When Frank went into the hospital, they all thought it might serve to memorialize Frank.

The people experienced multiple emotions. They loved their friend and worried about him, especially since they were not allowed to visit him. Another worry lurked in their minds: perhaps Frank had infected one of them — or more than one. Who among them might not have been fully vaccinated?

As it happened, Frank pulled through. When news of his dismissal reached his friends, they welcomed him back to the living by sending him "get well soon" cards. They waved to him and chatted whenever they met on the street. But they had no taste for dinner parties such as the mask-burning party they had had just before Frank left them. Helen finished her watercolor and called it "The Last Supper."

This was the "new normal."

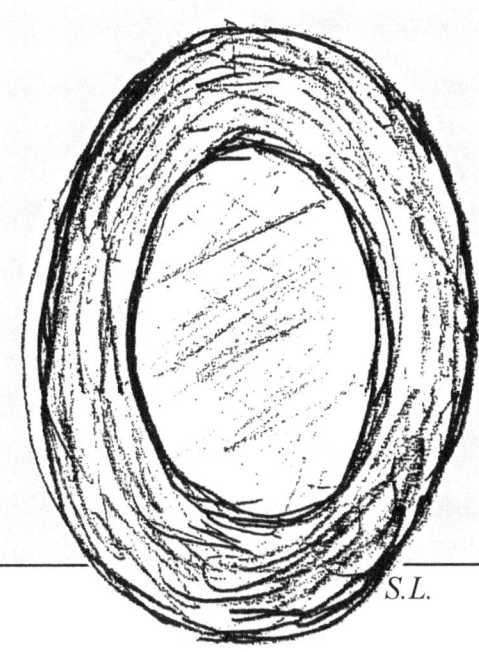

S.L.

Nothing
to anticipate

*F*or most of her life, Lydia Spencer enjoyed anticipating things to come. Generally, life turned out to be just what she anticipated and also just as pleasant as she foresaw it. That came to an end some years ago. She told herself, "There's nothing to anticipate."

One morning, before that happened, she awoke, yawned and stretched, then swung her legs over the side of the bed. After that burst of energy, she stayed seated. She had had a good sound sleep, but her first thought was how tired she felt. She even said it aloud: "I'm so tired!" It was a tiredness that sleep could not heal. She sighed and got to her feet slowly. She pulled off her nightgown and walked into the bathroom. There she was startled to see herself in the mirror. It's not that she did not expect to see herself. She knew the mirror was there and she would appear in it, but somehow, seeing herself in the moment was a sudden shock. Knowing that one is old is one thing, seeing how old is another.

She turned on the shower and let it warm up while she brushed her teeth. Then, she stepped into the shower and let the hot water pour over her. As she spread soapsuds over her body, she felt the flab of her upper arms, the sagging of her breasts and the loose crepe — like skin over her abdomen. Stepping out of the shower, she grabbed a towel and turned to the mirror. "Ah, one of nature's little blessings!" The steam of the shower had fogged the mirror over. She could only see a vague image of herself.

She dressed and went to the kitchen. Her day always began with talking. There was no one to talk to. She talked to herself. In fact, she talked to herself constantly. It was a way of pretending that she was not alone. She even answered herself from time to time. Today, for example, she said, "I'll just brew a pot of coffee." "That would be nice," she answered.

"You know, it is no wonder I feel old. Anybody with the name Lydia has to be old." "You're right. The last baby girl to be named Lydia must have been born more than eighty years ago." Lydia nodded in agreement: "That must have been me." That is how a typical day began. In fact, it continued that way the rest of the day and on into the next day.

Lydia Spencer and her husband, Theodore, moved into their apartment in the Happy Hills Retirement Home seventeen years ago. It seemed almost idyllic, and they were both pleased with the many services available to them. Indeed, they needed the nursing services within a few months' time. Theodore took sick. He had to be transferred to the nursing clinic. Lydia was left alone in the apartment but made two or three trips a day to the clinic to see to his needs. At lunchtime and supper, they sat together and talked. Gradually, his mind began to wander. He lost track of what he was saying and couldn't finish. One day, he had to struggle to remember who she was. It was as though he was drifting slowly and steadily away until he wasn't there anymore.

She quit making those long treks to the clinic. She stayed in the apartment by herself. She did crossword puzzles and took up needlepoint. She was good at it, but she also felt lonely — terribly lonely. One day, she said to herself, "What you need to do is to go outside, take a walk, breathe the fresh air." She thought about that for a while, decided that was what she should do — and she did. She repeated the exercise over the next two days. On the third day, she stopped at the great lounge where she plopped into an overstuffed armchair. It was very comfortable and she soon felt herself drifting off. In that half-sleep, she heard herself say, "I want to go home!" Hearing that, she jerked awake. "What," she demanded, "does that mean? 'I want to go home?'" For a long time, she thought about it, but it only led to her falling back to sleep.

The next thing she knew, a voice was gently calling her name. Groggily, she opened her eyes to see a nurse bending over her.

"We have been looking for you. We called your apartment several times, but you never answered. I'm glad I found you. Please come with me. I have news that requires our talking in a private place."

Saying that, the nurse, Mrs. Gregory, helped Lydia to her feet and led her into a small room just off the great lounge. It had a chair on each side of a table on which sat a box of Kleenex. Mrs. Gregory helped Lydia settle in one of the chairs while she went around to sit on the other side. Lydia thought to herself that this place looked the interrogation rooms in television police dramas. Mrs. Gregory gazed on Lydia for a few moments and then summoned up a sympathetic tone. "Mrs. Spencer, it is with a heavy heart that I must tell you that your dear husband, Theodore Spencer, has passed on to his heavenly award. I am so sorry to be the bearer of this sad news."

Staring straight ahead, Lydia said to herself, "Finally!"

There was a long pause. Mrs. Gregory cleared her throat. She pushed the tissue box toward Lydia. "You did hear me, did you not?" This time, Lydia nodded. "Now, we mostly follow certain protocols. Would you need to wait a day or two to deal with this, or may we start now?" Again. Lydia nodded. "To begin, we need to engage the services of a funeral home, unless you have already done so. Have you?" This time Lydia shook her head.

In a businesslike way, Mrs. Gregory took Lydia through all the decisions she needed to make, and Lydia obediently followed along. They established which funeral home, how the body would be transported there, whether the body should be cremated or buried, who should be alerted and what religious service should be conducted, and so forth. All this was quickly discussed and settled.

Lydia contacted her daughter, Audrey. She and her husband Roland and their twenty-six-year-old son agreed to come at once. That still required a few days. During that time, Lydia slept often and organized her papers as best she could. In between times, she caught herself saying again and again, "I want to go home."

All four of them attended a brief service in the chapel of the funeral home. Fortunately, Roland was an attorney and was able to take care of a number of legal matters. After a few days, the family returned home.

Lydia faced long empty days. She never felt so lonely. She had outlived her friends. She played card games with a few of the other residents of the home, but the relationships never went beyond the card games. Again, she would catch herself saying she wanted to go home. Now, she thought she knew what that meant. She no longer had anything to anticipate.

S.L.

The Short Life of

A Big Man

*H*e was already in the tenth grade, but Jamie Brewster's voice still hadn't changed. He had only a few stray hairs on his cheeks. What's more, he was big. He was almost as wide as he was tall. Tenth graders can be mean. They enjoyed making fun of him, and teased him mercilessly. Their favorite taunt was giving him nicknames such as "Rollypolly" and "His Great Chubbiness." They would call out to him with one such name and then "whoop and holler," slapping their knees. For his part, Jamie smiled and tried to look amused, but this caused him real pain.

His parents were not oblivious to his suffering. They consulted all sorts of medical experts from gastroenterologists, and endocrinologists, to psychiatrists. While some good came of it all, poor Jamie remained essentially the same. On the other hand, he started piano lessons at the early age of seven and had become very proficient. Of course, none of that meant anything to the hecklers he met every day in the halls of his school.

Coach Gerald Markham, the high school football coach, had noticed Jamie and the way his classmates treated him. He also noticed the boy's bulk. He decided that he might be able to help. He took Jamie aside and talked about how valuable he might be for the team. If he were to play center on offense, he could block to create an opening for the quarterback to break through the line. For a while, his classmates felt some admiration for him. Then, someone in the shower said, with a smirk, "Is that all you got, just that little stub?" Another chortled, saying, "Hey you, Stubby!" From that time until his college days, he was saddled with that nickname. When the girls found out how he got that name, they giggled and pointed at him. Coach Markham tried to intervene. He chastised the boys. He couldn't persuade Jamie to stay on the team. He dropped out.

He sensed a great release when he graduated and went on to college. Now, he could be his own man. He went to a university famous for its music school. There, he continued piano lessons. His teacher,

Professor Nalley, noticed his voice. In fact, he was fascinated by its special range and quality. He was a bona fide countertenor.

He passed the word on to his colleagues, Professor Amerson in vocal training and choral music, and Professor Tesser in the Theatre Department. Already in the season of plays was the musical Jesus Christ Superstar, and there was concern about casting the role of the priest Annas, who is supposed to be a countertenor. If all else fails, the thought was to use an alto singer in the role. Jamie was perfect, even if fitting him with a costume was difficult. There was an added benefit: Jamie showed a remarkable penchant for acting, which surprised even him. The show went into rehearsal under Tesser's stage direction and Amerson's music direction. The role of Annas is not a big one, but Jamie startled the audience with his convincing portrayal of the old priest. It was not just his voice. At the curtain call, he had to take three bows.

Before he got his degree, he was cast as a sort of buffoon in a television commercial. He played opposite a young beautiful woman, demonstrating the effects of bad eating habits and promoting a drug guaranteed to help with losing weight. He actually made money from that little stint of acting. From there, he went on to a professional revival of the play Of Mice and Men, in which he played the big, lumbering Lennie. The production was such a success, that it went on national tour. By the time the tour ended, several months later, he had become well known and was being offered parts.

Among those parts was one he truly enjoyed. He took on the role of Oliver Hardy in a remake of the movie The Music Box. The funny little actor who played Stan Laurel played so well opposite Jamie that the two comics came alive. In fact, the two actors shared an Oscar for their roles in that movie.

A few months after that, Jamie was on location working on a film. As is usual in those situations, there are long spans of time between one call and the next. Jamie could retire to his trailer while waiting.

One day, there was a knock on his door. He jumped up to answer it, thinking that it meant he had to return to the set. Instead, it was a man about his age who asked if he could talk with him. Jamie invited him in. The man took a seat on an awkward canvas chair while Jamie rolled onto the edge of his bed.

"How may I help you?"

"I just want you to know that I admire the career you have pursued for so many years now. I feel it an honor to have the chance to be a part of this project with you."

"Oh?" said Jamie. "What part do you have in this project?"

"Just a bit part, I'm afraid, but…" Charlie seemed uncomfortable. "Well, look, the writers have added a character to the cast. They've posted auditions for tomorrow. I thought maybe you could help."

Jamie eyed him closely. After a long pause, he said, "I think I know you. You're Charlie Nagel!"

"Yes! Charlie Nagel. That's me! We went to high school together."

"That's right. I remember!" Charlie was pleased. Then, Jamie continued, "I remember you very well. In fact, you were the one who gave me the nickname 'Stubby'."

Jamie looked at him for a long moment. Charlie squirmed in his chair. Then Jamie added, "Yes. Good old 'Can't-Get-It-Up Jamie Brewster'."

"I never said that. I swear."

"I know you didn't. Frankie Stewart said that. He said that and a lot of other nasty things.

"I am…sorry."

"Don't be. As you said, it was just hi-jinks in high school."

Charlie was astonished. "What?"

Jamie burst out laughing. When at last he recovered his breath, he said, "All that was a long time ago. Do you really think I would hold a grudge for all these years?"

"Ah! You were having me on." Charlie laughed in relief.

"Yes, I was having a bit of fun. Forgive me. I am reminded of all the pranks, schemes, and jokes we used to play in high school. You were a major perpetrator. You remember the time you found some school stationery and typed a note to our teacher, Mrs. Burns, informing her to dismiss class ten minutes early for an emergency faculty meeting? You even forged the principal's signature."

"I was never caught on that one. You remember the time somebody figured out how to open the opaque window at the girls' locker room just enough to watch them undressing?"

They went on in that vein, laughing at one story after another. After a while they had to stop just to catch a breath before the next wonderful event. Finally, they ran out of stories to tell.

Charlie panted as he exclaimed, "Ah, those were the days, my friend."

Jamie rolled back on his bed. "Those days are long gone…thank God!"

In the quiet that followed, Charlie struggled to get out of the canvas chair. He straightened himself then helped Jamie to sit up. Charlie became serious, as he remembered why he had come to Jamie's trailer in the first place. "Say, Jamie."

"Yes?"

"Look. I came here to ask a favor of you."

"What is it?"

"Well, as I told you, they're having auditions tomorrow for the role of the new character. I thought maybe you could put in a good word for me, sort of in honor of our long friendship. They'd listen to you. Maybe you could write a letter recommending me. Could you do that?"

"Nope."

"Why not?"

"Well, if there was a call for a high school joker, maybe, but I don't know you as an actor. I don't have anything to go on."

Charlie was stunned. He stared at Jamie, and then blurted out, "So, Your Great Chubbiness has spoken."

"What did you say?"

"You really haven't forgiven me, have you, Stubby?"

Jamie couldn't believe his ears. "I forgave you years ago. This is not about retaliation for something you may have done back in high school. It has to do with professional ethics. I can recommend only those with whom I have worked or whose work I have seen."

Charlie wagged his head. "What a load of crap! I'll show you. I'll go to that audition and I'll get the part. You'll see." Saying that, Charlie went out the door.

As it happened, Charlie did go to the audition, but he did not get the part. Jamie turned in a powerful performance for the film. It was so powerful that critics universally gave it high praise. Jamie never knew that. At the age of forty-two, he suffered a fatal heart attack and died just before the film was released. He simply could no longer carry the heavy weight of his body.

A Precise
Couple

*A*fter sixty-two years of marriage, Bertrand and Myrtle Byran had developed the seeming ability to read each other's minds. They scarcely needed to talk. They had a remarkable capacity to merge their efforts in any task they might undertake. For example, breakfast each morning ran with precision. She cooked bacon and eggs, prepared the toast, brewed the coffee and placed it all on a platter. Meanwhile, he set out the items on the dining table with placemats, utensils, napkins, glasses and cups. It all went like clockwork, their duties merging so precisely that they sat down at the very same moment. Clearing and cleaning up at the end of the meal went forward with the same quiet precision. After that, they divided the newspaper between themselves. He took the front section, the opinion page, and the sports news. She took the living section, the society news and the arts columns. Then in unison, they sat in their respective easy chairs. It was a pleasant, well-ordered life.

One Tuesday morning, this routine began to take a new twist. It started off innocuously enough. As usual, they would each make a quick remark on a news item of one sort or another. It might be a story about a teenager stealing groceries or a woman being deported to her native country, or a shooting in another part of town. They would read to one another, leading to short comments such as "What is this world coming to?" or "Seems like everybody has a gun!" or simply "Tut tut tut!"

After a quiet pause, Bertrand looked over at Myrtle. She had her eyes closed, causing him to ask, "Did you fall asleep?" When she did not answer, he uttered, "Myrtle?"

"What?"

"Are you all right?"

She sat up straight. "Just resting my eyes. I was reading the obituaries."

"Why? Just to be sure your name's not there?" Bertrand chuckled at his little joke.

"No, no. I read here that two people died yesterday and they shared the very same birthday."

"Remarkable."

"What's more, they were exactly the same age."

"Um." Bertrand returned to his newspaper.

After a few minutes, Myrtle put the paper down. "I am a year older than they were. Do you think it means anything? A portent or so?"

"You mean, your name will appear in tomorrow's obits?"

After a brief pause, she said quietly, "Yes."

"Of course not!" Bertrand went back behind his paper.

Myrtle tried to stare a hole in his newspaper. He sensed it and put the paper down. They were now staring at each other. Myrtle broke the silence: "You feel something in your head?"

"Yes, but I can't describe it."

"Ever since we sat down after breakfast I have felt as though my mind were emptying, becoming lighter."

"Yes, that's it. Exactly." Just as had happened throughout their life together, they shared a sense, a feeling, a thought. This was a little different. It was not just sharing; it was as if a force had come into their being, a strong and undeniable force. They nodded as if in assent.

"I think I know what is happening," Myrtle said quietly

"So do I," said Bertrand, equally quietly.

They each turned toward one another with a faint smile and a loving look. Then they settled back in their chairs. They closed their eyes and they each let out a slow breath.

Later that day, the two were found in their easy chairs, the Tuesday edition of the newspaper at their feet.

Santa
Stops By

Stevie Messer was just six-years-old, but he felt he had learned many things about the world. Some of those things he knew because his older brother, Kevin, showed him and answered his questions. Kevin was six years older and could explain many things. From Kevin, for example, Stevie knew that the sun always sets in the west so he could see the sunset if he looked to the west, and west was always in the direction of the house of his friend, Jack. Kevin surprised Stevie by telling him that the sun was not moving to the west. Instead, the earth was turning toward the east, making the sun seem to move the opposite direction. Stevie wondered about many things. Often Kevin knew the answer. On one occasion, Stevie thought it strange that enough water could be in the sky that it could come down on earth in torrents. How did all that water get there? Kevin explained to him about evaporation and condensation. He grew to trust Kevin to have the answers

For some weeks before Christmas, Stevie had been thinking about Santa Claus, wondered how he could deliver presents to him in the middle of the night. He examined the fireplace and the chimney and thought there was no way he could come down that narrow shaft. Kevin was very informative. He explained that Santa knew all about the houses he was to visit and he had a plan for each one. Kevin added Santa always appreciated some help. Stevie could, for example, open the window beside the fireplace just a crack. Then, Santa could lift up the sash and bring the presents in. Kevin also pointed out that Santa would be grateful for any cookies Stevie might place just inside that window. Cookies would surely give him the energy he needed for his long journey.

Stevie dutifully followed these suggestions. There was a batch of cookies in the kitchen. Stevie put four of them on a plate. Kevin helped Stevie to write a note to go with the cookies with these simple words: "For you." Then Stevie placed the plate and the note by the window and cracked it open very little. Mother came and told him it was time to go to bed. He had to do it. Santa will come only after he falls asleep. Feeling pleased with himself, he climbed the stairs with Mother, who tucked him into bed and turned out the light. It seemed to take forever to get to sleep.

Still, he must have gone off into slumber because he awoke in the morning with the sunbeams slanting across the room. He ran downstairs as fast as he could, right to that window. There were new presents lying next to the window, but what really caught his attention was two cookies that remained on the plate. With them was the same piece of paper he used for his note. There were new words on the paper. He could not quite read them.

He took the paper and ran to Kevin's room. "Look. Kevin! Look! Santa left a note for me. See?" He held it out Kevin who opened one eye. "See?" Stevie went on. "See, he wrote on the paper I left with the cookies. What does it say?"

Kevin smiled. "Let's have a look." He took the paper from Stevie. He studied it for a few moments. Then, he announced, "It says, 'I saved these for you.' What does that mean?"

Stevie smiled broadly. "I know! I know! He ate two cookies and left the other two for me. Come on. I'll show you." Stevie ran out, back to the window. Kevin, somewhat groggily, followed him.

"See?" Stevie pointed to the two cookies. "That's what it means. He left them for me. Do you want one? I can share." He gave Kevin one and the two boys sat down on the floor and ate their cookies.

Later that morning, after the family had breakfast and opened presents, Stevie dozed off, pleased with his gifts of a new toy car, a board game and a book. He hadn't slept long before Kevin woke him, saying, "I want to show you something. Wake up. We have to go outside." Saying that, he handed Stevie his winter coat.

Stevie pulled on the coat and followed his brother outside to the window that Stevie had cracked open for Santa. It was cold and Stevie wanted to back inside. "Wait. I want you to see this," Kevin insisted.

He pointed to the ground. "See those prints in the snow?

"What sort of prints?" asked Stevie.

"Look closely. What do you see? There are three kinds of prints."

Stevie looked. There were three kinds of prints in the snow.

There on the ground were hoof prints and runner prints and boot prints. Those boot prints went right up to the window and back to the runner prints. He was amazed. He looked at Kevin and back at the prints. He was so grateful to his brother. This was clear proof that Santa had been there.

Stevie wanted his friend Jack, who lived to the west, to see all this evidence. He went and told Jack, who had to see it for himself. The two of them stood there admiring all the tracks in the snow. Jack wanted to know how Kevin knew to look for signs of Santa's visit. Kevin said it was simple: Santa had to come in through that window.

Later, when Stevie and Jack were older, Kevin showed them what he had done. He used a four-by-eight piece of plywood and dragged it over the snow to the window. He laid it down and then worked backwards. Using a couple of tin cans, he made the reindeer hoof prints in the show. Then, using big boots, he made tracks to the window and back to the sleigh. Finally, he pulled the plywood away, smoothing out his own footprints in the snow, meanwhile indenting the snow with the "runners."

Stevie and Jack stared blankly at Kevin for a moment. Then they broke into wide smiles and applauded Kevin for his wondrous work.

S.L.

www.ingramcontent.com/pod-product-compliance
Lightning Source LLC
Chambersburg PA
CBHW081207170626
46811CB00011B/3340